The Beach Fai~~

*How a retired tooth fairy becomes the first
beach fairy on the Outer Banks of North Carolina.*

"K" Stone

Story by **"K" Stone**

with Illustrations by **Mary Lee Dunn**

For:

All who believe in things that cannot be seen.

To: Sutton

I can't wait to bring treats to someone as special as you!

♡+,
The Beach Fairy

"Zippity, zappity, zing!" said Tessie, a tooth fairy, as she waved her magic wand to zap herself to the Wright Memorial Bridge leading to the Outer Banks beaches. She noticed the tall poles cradling ospreys' nests. She decided to sleep in an empty one so she could rethink her big decision to retire to this coastal paradise like lots of people did. She needed a change, and she had always wanted to do something no other fairy had ever done. She held her dreams close to her heart as she curled up and slept soundly until the light of day appeared in the Carolina blue sky.

The next morning Tessie was ready for her new adventure. She jumped into the air to begin her flight across the bridge and pressed her tiny self against the strong breezes coming off the waters of the sound. Tessie flew a few feet above one of the many colorful cars packed with kids and parents headed for a beach vacation. When it turned left at Kitty Hawk Pier, she did too. It was only a moment before she noticed a chubby, playful whale weathervane perched on top of a light gray cottage. "Children must live there!" she said happily. She swooped down on the beach across from the house and found a cozy spot among the sea oats to call home.

The next day, Tessie was taking an afternoon snooze below the wooden walkway that leads to the beach. She heard two loud voices over the sound of the surf.

"I love the way the sand tickles my toes, KK," an excited little girl shouted.

"I do too, Georgia," said the older woman who must be her grandmother. Tessie became an invisible pixy spy flying close enough to watch Georgia play.

First, she saw Georgia and her grandmother take turns burying each other's feet in the wet sand. Then, they built sandcastles and decorated them with feathers and shells Georgia had collected on the beach. Suddenly, Georgia raced to the ocean's edge and plopped down. The little spy from Fairyland flitted there too just in time to hear Georgia say, "Let's feed the ocean some dinner, KK!"

"Okay, how 'bout some meatballs!" KK answered. They made sandy meatballs and tossed them into the splashing waves.

Tessie noticed delight on Georgia's face as she sat enjoying the beach's music. Tessie realized that she liked listening to the gurgling of the foam and the hissing of the waves flowing back into the sea just as much as Georgia did.

"The ocean is so big and beautiful," Georgia said.

KK answered, "That's because it is filled with so much life."

"It is my favorite place in the whole world," Georgia exclaimed. The moment Tessie saw Georgia's heart drawn in the sand, she drew one with fairy dust. Tessie loved the beach too. She decided she would become Georgia's beach fairy first, and then maybe one day she could make lots of children happy again.

In the midst of whirling fairy dust, Tessie began to change. Her wand now had a starfish on its tip, and she dressed herself in stylish beach clothes with lots of jewelry from the sea. She felt pretty and proud.

When KK and Georgia walked hand in hand off the beach, the Beach Fairy followed them. The two climbed the steps to the cottage with the whale weathervane perched on top. Now, Tessie knew just where to find Georgia when it was the perfect time for her first beach fairy visit.

At bedtime Tessie flew over to the beach house and heard Georgia crying, "I'm scared in the room by myself, and I can't fall asleep!"

KK tried to comfort Georgia, but she could not until she felt the tickle of Tessie's fairy dust in her nose. She sneezed loudly and said, "Georgia, if you don't get out of bed again, I bet the Beach Fairy will leave you a surprise under your pillow."

"What's the Beach Fairy?" Georgia asked.

Tessie quickly sprinkled more fairy dust on KK before she could answer. "She's a retired Tooth Fairy with big dreams. She brings surprises to good children on beach vacations. Just go to sleep now, and you may find out in the morning." When Georgia was in dreamland, the Beach Fairy eased a lollipop under Georgia's pillow.

Sure enough, when Georgia felt under her pillow the next morning, she found the luscious lemon lollipop. Then, she raced to her grandmother's room waving the candy and yelling, "May I eat it now?"

"Fine, but you must promise to eat all your breakfast."

"I promise, I promise!" she shouted. And she did!

The little Beach Fairy, who sat close by, was thrilled by Georgia's delight. Tessie knew that being a Beach Fairy was exactly what she wanted to do.

After cleaning the breakfast dishes, KK and Georgia went to swing on the front porch. KK taught Georgia "The Beach Fairy Song" to sing every night before lights out. Georgia asked, "Will this song make the Beach Fairy come again?"

"Let's just wait and see," said KK. The next night Georgia did not get up from her bed a single time. They sang "The Beach Fairy Song," and KK tucked Georgia in. There was nothing under her pillow the following morning. When Georgia went to KK's room, she asked, "Why didn't the Beach Fairy come?"

"Maybe she doesn't visit every night because she likes to surprise you."

The following day, the Beach Fairy saw Georgia and KK loading their car for a trip to Jockey's Ridge to climb the highest sand dune on the east coast. She wanted to explore too, so she followed them. The Beach Fairy was amazed to see the hang gliders high over the steep slope. She giggled with delight as the many children rolled down the dune again and again until their pockets were bulging with sand.

Even though Georgia and KK were very tired that night, they walked on the beach just before bedtime. They couldn't see well in the twilight, but they spotted an occasional sand crab crawling to find safety. As they walked off the beach, Georgia told KK how much she hoped the Beach Fairy would visit again. Tessie was there perched on the rail listening with a big smile on her little face.

KK did not hear a peep from Georgia after singing "The Beach Fairy Song" that night. When Tessie showed up, her glow lit the bedroom just enough for her to be certain Georgia was asleep. She magically slipped a surprise under her pillow without a single sound and sprinkled fairy dust on Georgia just as she had on KK.

Georgia was thrilled the next morning to discover a mini flashlight. Now, she would be able see the sand crabs dash about on the beach after dark. Georgia knew that the Beach Fairy must have been close by last night since she had brought the perfect gift.

Georgia raced to show KK her new flashlight. She shouted, "I am so lucky to have a beach fairy! Her visits are so fun! I wish everyone had a beach fairy!" Georgia ran to draw the Beach Fairy a picture showing lots of beach fairies on beaches everywhere. The fairy dust had worked its magic again!

Georgia placed the drawing under her pillow and fell asleep. Soon, the Beach Fairy flew into Georgia's room and saw the paper sticking out from under the pillow. She made a sparkly check in the smiley-face box immediately. Tessie also wanted more tooth fairies to become beach fairies. Her dreams were coming true!

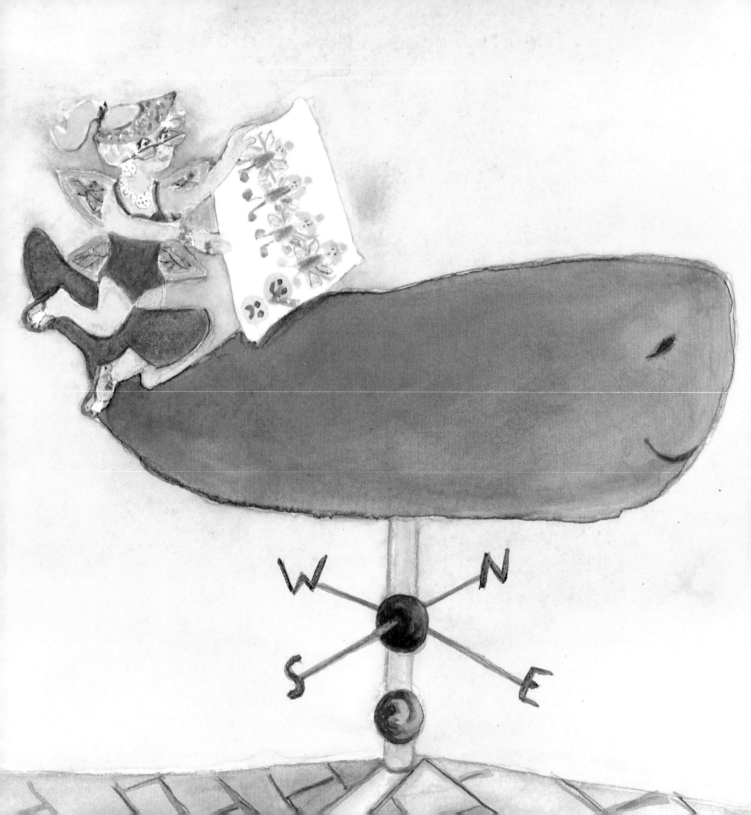

The bright sun coming in the window woke Georgia early the next morning. She reached for the note and beamed when she saw the smiley face checked with shiny pink fairy dust. She decided to leave the note under her pillow for the Beach Fairy.

Georgia's week at the beach with her grandmother had passed by quickly. As they rode out of the driveway later in the morning, Georgia gazed up to wave bye-bye to Chubby, the whale weathervane. Right on the top of his tail sat Tessie, the very first beach fairy ever. She was proudly holding Georgia's picture.

Georgia wondered out loud, "KK, do you think more beach fairies will be here the next time we come to the beach?"

"I bet they will," KK answered. "All it takes to attract a beach fairy is to love the beach, to go to bed on beach vacations without a fuss, and to believe in things that cannot be seen.

GLOSSARY

Jockey's Ridge – the largest sand dune on the East Coast

Kitty Hawk Pier – the landmark fishing pier located at MP 1

Osprey – a large hawk that feeds only on fish

Outer Banks (OBX) – the 200-mile string of barrier islands along the North Carolina coast

Retire – when a person stops working and has time to follow dreams

Sand Dune – a hill or ridge of drifted sand

Sea Glass – chemically and physically weathered glass found on beaches, often used to make lovely jewelry

Sea Oats – a species of grass that grows along the East Coast

Tooth Fairy – the generous fairy that visits snaggle-toothed children when they lose their baby teeth and leaves them money under their pillows

Weathervane – a free-swinging device that shows which direction the wind is blowing

Wright Memorial Bridge – the 3 mile bouncy bridge that crosses the Currituck Sound and leads to the Outer Banks

THE BEACH FAIRY SONG

Sing to the tune of "Mr. Sandman" by Pat Ballard

Little Beach Fairy, bring me a dream.
Make it the best that I've ever seen.
Give it some action and lots of color.
And I won't wake until it's all over.

Little Beach Fairy, bring me a treat.
Make it a toy or something to eat.
I'll be so brave and sleep without fear.
And when I wake, I'll know you were here!

Lyrics by "K" Stone

Acknowledgements

Manon Romash - a former student who utilized her expert computer skills to help me self-publish

Ginny Matish - a forever friend who facilitated and encouraged my desire to write

Debbie Baxter - a dear fellow-writer and former English teacher who edited my story

Made in the USA
Middletown, DE
14 November 2016